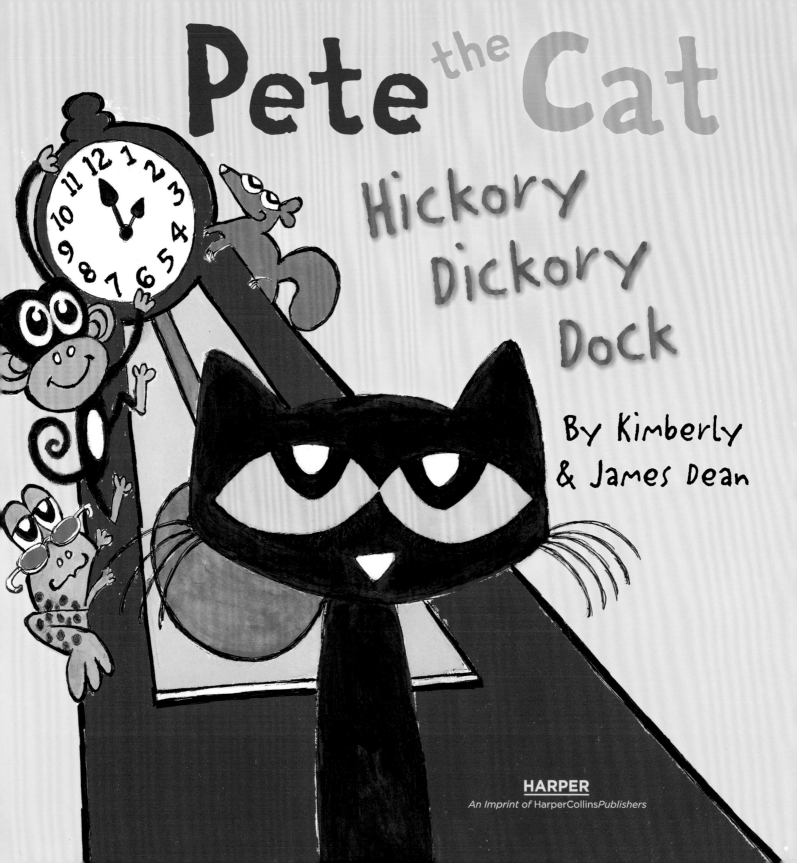

Pete the Cat

Hickory Dickory Dock

By Kimberly & James Dean

HARPER
An Imprint of HarperCollinsPublishers

Hickory
dickory
dock.

Pete the Cat
went up the clock.

The clock struck one. Pete went down.
Hickory dickory dock.

Tick tock,
tick tock,
tick tock,
tick tock.

Hickory
dickory
dock.

Grumpy Toad went up the clock.

The clock struck two.
Grumpy Toad went down.
Hickory dickory dock.

Tick tock,
tick tock,
tick tock,
tick tock.

Hickory
dickory
dock.

Squirrel went up the clock.

The clock struck three.
Squirrel went down.
Hickory dickory dock.

Tick tock,
tick tock,
tick tock,
tick tock.

Hickory dickory dock.

Bob went up the clock.

The clock struck four.
Bob went down.
Hickory dickory dock.

Tick tock,
tick tock,
tick tock,
tick tock.

Hickory dickory dock.

Marty went up the clock.

The clock struck five.
Marty went down.
Hickory dickory dock.

Tick tock,
tick tock,
tick tock,
tick tock.

Hickory dickory dock.